ESCAPE
and
RESCUE

ESCAPE
and
RESCUE

A NOVELLA

A story of love, grace, and redemption.

The Redemption Series

BOOK 1

Sheila Daniel

XULON ELITE

Xulon Press Elite
2301 Lucien Way #415
Maitland, FL 32751
407.339.4217
www.xulonpress.com

Paperback ISBN-13: 978-1-6628-2961-1
Ebook ISBN-13: 978-1-6628-2962-8

Dedication

This book is dedicated to all the precious women who, like Sophia, find themselves trapped in abusive relationships.

May God's love, grace, and redemption be yours.

Acknowledgements

So many wonderful people joined in the writing of this book. Some offered a gentle push when fear tried to halt me. Others coaxed me to take one more step when the trek before me seemed too daunting.

From prayer warriors to cheerleaders. From strangers to family and friends. From launch team members to beta readers and critique group members. This has been a joint effort from the very beginning.

I can't begin to name you all, nor can I thank you enough. I only hope my words, though inadequate, will somehow help you grasp the extent of my gratitude. I thank you from the bottom of my heart.

Also, many thanks to Xulon Press for giving me this opportunity. And thank you, God, for opening the door and nudging me to walk through. I may have never done it, otherwise (but You already knew that, didn't You?).

To my husband –
Your love and support have always breathed life into my dreams. Thank you for being my biggest fan.

To my children and grandchildren –
You bring sunshine into all of my days. I am so grateful to be called your Mom and Mim.

To my parents – Thank you for always believing in me, even when I had little belief in myself.

To Gee – Thank you for staying close and cheering me on. I can't imagine life without you in it.

To Kenny – If you were here, you'd give me the biggest hug. One day, I'll collect on that hug. Until then…

"Then you will call upon Me and come and pray to Me, and I will listen to you. And you will seek Me and find Me when you search for Me with all your heart" (Jer. 29:12-13 NASB).

Table of Contents

Preface

A NOTE FROM THE AUTHOR

I had not planned to write this book.

Not now. Not anytime soon. Maybe never.

But as is often the case, God's plans for me exceeded my own.

While skimming through an endless list of unopened emails, one email in particular grabbed my attention. *A writing contest*. I read through the guidelines; the deadline was merely days away. Could I pull this off in time? The planner and plotter in me tossed everything aside and decided to give it a try.

Much to my surprise – but not to God's – I won the contest. That win landed me my very own publishing contract. For the book I had not yet written. For the book I had not consciously planned to write. For the book you now hold in your hands.

God is good.

You see, God knew exactly what I needed. I had prayed for years over this nudging to write. I had asked for His guidance. I had asked that His will be revealed. Slowly and methodically, He began to answer those prayers; He opened a door I could have never opened on my own.

I am forever grateful.

CHAPTER 1

The Departure

The door slammed so intensely I expected it to break loose from its hinges. I could no longer see his face, yet I shuddered to imagine the anger unveiled within it. His words were usually few, but his countenance spoke volumes. Flames from his dark eyes had grazed me one too many times. When his anger magnified to this degree, it never led to anything good. It was time to get out of his way. It was time to quiet the children.

In one swift motion, I placed Roger on my hip and reached for Clara's hand. We made our way down the hall, through the living quarters, and to the outer terrace in record time. Though beautiful, it wasn't the best place for occupying children—not for any length of time, anyway. Had I been smart, I would have stashed away a few toys for days like this. Pre-packaged crackers and juice boxes would've been nice, too. *Why is it I never think of such things until it's too late?*

"Mommy, can we go for a walk on the trail? Just until Daddy feels better?"

Oh, my sweet Clara. So many times I'd made excuses for this man she thought to be her daddy. "No, honey. We need to stay close in case Daddy needs us."

She frowned, but only for a moment. Her eyes took on a new sparkle as she surveyed the wide-open terrace. Other than a sparse collection of terra cotta pots abandoned at the house's edge, the terrace was void of any obstacles.

"That's okay, Mommy. I'll practice my skipping, instead." And off she went, seemingly unbothered by another no.

How did I end up with such a sweet girl? I watched as she moved with ease, skipping and twirling to the far end of the terrace and back again. In this moment, she was free to be the innocent little girl she should be. Enjoying life without worry or fear crouching at her door. This calm innocence would be short-lived today, the same as most other days.

Pulling him close, I snuggled Roger to my chest before his growing impatience turned into all-out fury. Within moments, his thirst would be satisfied and he'd be resting peacefully, without a care in the world. *Oh, how I wished to be in that place with him, in that state of satisfaction, contentment, peace. Will I ever know such a place? Will such an existence ever be mine? Oh, Sophia, how did you get yourself into such a mess?*

The squeaking of the outer gate at the far end of the quarter-mile driveway interrupted my thoughts. The gate opened its mouth to a familiar black limousine. I could not see the limo from where I sat on the terrace, but it had come and gone with such regularity the sound of it embedded in my mind. Sometimes, its arrival left my husband in a jovial state. Other times, it brought out the tyrant in him. Oh, how I hoped it would improve his mood today. Moments later, I knew better.

"Sophia! Get in here!"

I scrambled to my feet, jarring Roger awake. Trying to quiet him while grabbing hold of Clara, I rushed the three of us inside. Without a word, I led the children into the large bedroom they shared. Clara knew the routine. She grabbed Roger's pacifier and took her seat on a mat in the far corner of the room. Placing Roger across her lap, I kissed her forehead and tried to ignore the fear settling into her eyes.

"Sophia!"

"Coming, Marcus! Coming."

"When I call you, I expect you to come without delay!"

I paused before stepping over the threshold, knowing my next move would land me face to face with fierce opposition. He barreled toward me, eyes blazing and jaw clenched. Using my arm as a makeshift shield, I closed my eyes tightly and cowered beneath the weight of his fury.

He shoved me across the room, wielding my body into the nearest wall. Grabbing a handful of hair, he yanked me to my feet and scowled at me. For a moment I thought his tantrum had ended. Instead, the backside of his hand met my cheekbone, forcing me to my knees.

"Perhaps next time, you'll come when you're called."

Using both hands to steady myself, I pushed the pain aside and willed myself to stand.

"I'm sorry, honey. What is it you need?" The words rolled off my tongue like a well-rehearsed movie script. My voice, no trace of fear or fight. My tone, perfected by the opportunities I'd been given to practice my script. I understood what made matters worse, what prolonged the beatings and what hurried them along. Through it all, I had somehow learned to survive. *How long had I been living in survival mode?*

"Pack my belongings! I'll be going away for a few days. And don't forget my casual shoes this time!"

I made my way into my husband's closet, a large room filled with enough clothing to dress an army of men. *Sophia, choose wisely what he'll want*—knowing all along it mattered not what I chose. He would find something wrong with my selections, warranting me a scolding—or worse—upon his return. Of this, I could be certain.

I had the process of packing down to an art. I folded and stacked a variety of shirts and pants into the largest of his suitcases, arranging them into sets based upon color and texture. Matching accessories, such as ties, belts, and socks were strategically placed within the bag's upper compartment. Shoes and undergarments were situated into separate bags, per his liking.

Within ten minutes, I had him fully packed. After carrying each bag to its allotted space by the front door, I remained in sight, afraid my absence would provoke him further. Present, but silent—that's what he expected of me. I stood nearby, trying to keep my hands from wringing the bottom of my shirt into a messy wad—an action that would no doubt annoy him.

Twenty minutes later, the familiar black limousine carried him and his companions down the drive, out the gate, and on their way. I cared not about their intended destination. I only cared that he was gone.

With the closing of the gate, I breathed a quiet sigh of relief and made my way back to my children. Sweet Clara, sitting up straight, as if at attention. She burst into tears as I walked into the room. Taking Roger from her arms, I pulled her trembling body into mine. We remained in this stance until her shaking finally subsided. Blinking away the tears welling up in my own eyes, I turned her face toward mine.

"Clara, everything is going to be okay. Mommy promises. What do you say we go bake ourselves some peanut butter cookies?"

"Okay, Mommy."

But this time, the smile on her face didn't mask the sadness in her beautiful brown eyes.

Seeing my own sadness mirrored in the eyes of my daughter brought me to a place I hadn't been in a long time: a place of intentional prayer. Silent, but still somehow soothing. *Lord, this cannot go on. Won't you please help us find a way out?*

CHAPTER 2

The Plan Uncovered

I awakened with my heart racing and my fists clenched. It took a moment to remember—only the children and I were home. I tossed my blanket to the side and slowly lifted my aching body out of bed. Sliding my feet into my worn slippers, I stepped into the bathroom and peered into the full-length mirror hanging beside the shower door.

Though I could do nothing to stop the beatings, I would do my best to hide the evidence they left behind. It was bad enough that my children had to witness such travesty; I certainly didn't want my bruised body to become a visible reminder.

I winced as I pushed my arms through an oversized top. Slipping my legs into loose sweatpants, I surveyed my reflection once more. Convinced my bruised shoulders and ribs were adequately covered, I headed down the hallway to the children's room.

Peeking inside, I could see that Roger had crawled out of his toddler bed and joined Clara in her twin-size canopy bed. Snuggling closely together, they almost appeared as one. They slept soundly, as if knowing today would be a good day.

I had to admit, Marcus's absence did usher in a long overdue semblance of peace. Though I could never fully relax, I would choose to be grateful; I would do all I could to make these next few days joyful for my children.

But first, I had some investigating to do.

I didn't bother checking the office door. It always remained locked, even when Marcus was home, working within it. But there was one thing my husband, in all his controlling, did not know. I possessed the key he had carelessly left inside his pants pocket months ago. I found it while loading clothes into the washing machine. Somehow, I had managed to dodge his attention as he retraced his steps a few days later. No doubt he thought me too fearful and ignorant to have done anything with it. For once, he was wrong.

I had hidden the key in the back of the cupboard, buried deep within a large canister of surplus flour. I kept this extra flour on hand in case I ran short in my everyday supply. I had made the mistake of running out of flour once early in our marriage. That mistake left me with a bruise so deep it took weeks to heal. It seems my husband doesn't do well when told there is no flour for his favorite homemade bread. I had no idea at the time that an extra canister of flour would come in so handy.

Holding the canister over the kitchen sink to minimize the mess, I retrieved the odd-shaped key from its hiding place, rinsed and dried it well, and headed toward my husband's study. Though there was no one home to police me, I moved cautiously as I opened the door and surveyed the vast room.

If not for the large windows opposite his desk, the room would be a dungeon. Dark paneled walls, dark furniture, dark carpet. Even the décor was void of color. But the darkness enveloping this room went beyond the décor. Darkness was somehow a part of this room. It felt as if evil itself encircled me, it's breath hot upon the nape of my neck.

Summoning all the bravery I could muster, I entered the room and moved closer to his desk, knowing his most urgent business would be hidden within one of its three drawers. I opened each drawer, knowing not what I was looking for yet nervous about what I might find.

I ran my hand over the tops of the folders, skimming the tabs of each. After removing each folder from its assigned drawer, I positioned the folders into three separate stacks across the floor. Working on the floor wouldn't be nearly as comfortable, especially in my bruised state, but I couldn't risk disturbing the layout of his desk.

Beginning with the pile nearest me, I started skimming through each folder. Quickly, but efficiently, I scanned the material. It wouldn't be long before the children awakened. I didn't dare attempt this task with children underfoot.

An hour and a half later, I began thumbing through the contents of the final folder. My focus wavered; so far, I had seen nothing of concern. All the folders contained what appeared to be legitimate records relevant to my husband's rental business. Nothing seemed out of the ordinary.

Knowing that time was short, I hurriedly flipped through the remaining papers. Just when I thought all was clear, I caught sight of what appeared to be initials scribbled in the top right-hand corner of a single page. *C and R.* Could these initials be for Clara and Roger?

Holding my spot with my left hand, I pulled the page closer. My right index finger made its way down the page, stopping abruptly at the words I had feared finding.

"One girl child, age 5 1/2 years. One boy child, age 2 1/2 years. To be surrendered in payment of any and all outstanding debts."

My mind questioned what I had read.

One girl? One boy? In payment of outstanding debts?

A thick fog enveloped me. I could see nothing but the words dangling before me. It seemed as if those few words had jumped from the page, consuming the only breathable air available to me. My heart pounded. My thoughts jumbled together. I couldn't move. *What could this mean?*

Sounds drifted in through the doorway and out again. A child whimpering. Another tiny voice consoling.

Slowly, the fog began to dissipate. My mind could hear these drifting sounds, but they seemed miles from me, not simply down the hall. I fought to reclaim my senses. To focus on something other than this page. I struggled, somehow knowing I must redirect my eyes so that my mind could better engage. I breathed deeply. My ability to reason returned. Clarity set in. *What in the world was my husband planning?*

Roger's whimpering, now a full-on wail, jerked me back to reality. *Roger.* Though more than capable of drinking regular milk from a sippy cup, he still preferred a short breastfeeding in the mornings and at nap time. With his third birthday drawing near, I probably should have weaned him by now. But since neither of us felt ready, I would nurse him a bit longer. Weaning could wait for another day.

With shaking hands, I took one last glance at the paper and slid it back inside its folder. After placing the folder into the appropriate stack, I lifted each pile carefully, returning them, one by one, to the correct drawer. A glimpse around the room assured me that everything was in its rightful place. Locking the door behind me, I ran to my children.

"Mommy's coming, Roger; Clara, Mommy's coming."

* * *

Marcus would be home soon; I felt certain of it. He said he'd be gone a few days, and those few days had long since passed. The calm I had hoped to feel in his absence vanished shortly after his departure.

Since uncovering the paper brandishing my children's initials, dread and fear had become my constant companions. One awful scenario after another held my thoughts captive. *What horrific circumstances would my children face in the days ahead? If those words meant what I feared they meant, what could I do? How could I thwart my husband's evil plans?*

With so many key relationships in my life severed, would there be anyone willing to help? If by some slim chance we escaped this house and distanced ourselves from this property, would we find anyone worthy of our trust?

Was it possible that Marcus's influence had reached those living outside these walls? Could the neighbors be trusted to offer us sanctuary, or would they turn us over to him? And without intervention, how could I stop the inevitable?

In that moment, my thoughts settled into the hardest reality of all. *There was no help coming for me or my children.*

CHAPTER 3

Past Mistakes, Present Trouble

I had allowed him to move us to this remote community where the nearest homes stood miles from our own. He had convinced me a fresh start would do us good. He insisted what he wanted more than anything was for us to be together. Everything would be better without outside opinions and interference from others. And I had fallen for it, believing a fairy tale ending could be mine after all.

All of this, coupled with the wooing pace of small-town living, the beauty of nature nestled within the nearby mountain range, and the endless supply of fresh, unpolluted air led me to believe there was no place better to raise my children.

Acting on impulse, I agreed to move three hours from home, neglecting to whisper a word of it to family or friends, refusing to see my true reality, living as if all the hard things would simply work themselves out.

Why hadn't I talked it over with someone other than Marcus? Why had I been so set on listening to no one but him?

* * *

The last time I spoke to my parents, we had gathered at my childhood home for Mom's birthday. Surprised that Marcus agreed to go, I felt like a child anticipating Christmas morning.

When we first arrived, all the good I had hoped for in that visit seemed within reach. We'd been there about an hour when Mom and I began setting the table and chatting about how much the children had grown.

Stepping back, I admired the beautiful bouquet of fresh sunflowers posing on its usual stage at the table's center. Though the stems had been trimmed considerably, the flowers stood tall and confident in the green-tinted mason jar I'd given Mom years ago.

Sunflowers had always been her favorite; no doubt, Dad had made a deliberate trip into town to buy these for her special day. This thought made me both happy and sad. *Why was my relationship with Marcus not like that of my parents?*

Glancing into the living room at the only two men I had ever loved, I couldn't help but wonder, *How can they be so different? Why is there no warmth in Marcus's eyes when he looks at me? Why is there still warmth in Dad's eyes when he looks at Mom, even after all these years?*

I turned my attention to Mom, moving effortlessly through the kitchen. Her demeanor was always pleasant. Her words always soft and carefully chosen. *Did she and Dad ever feel truly angry with one another? Did she ever feel unhappy in her marriage? Had she ever felt trapped like I sometimes do?*

Brushing my feelings aside, I called the children into the house. With sudsy washcloths waiting, I guided them toward the sink to ready them for the meal. Judging from the amount of dirt covering their hands and faces, they had made good use of their outdoor play time. A warm sensation filled my heart. My children were making memories in the same back yard where I had played so happily all those years ago.

"Clara, why don't you sit here by Nana?" I scooted her chair under the table and brushed hair out of her eyes. Taking my spot next to Clara, I placed Roger in my lap and hoped he would sit still without a highchair to strap him into. *Please let our visit continue to go well.*

The conversation over dinner began innocently enough. Dad and Marcus discussed the weather and fishing and the declining economy. Mom and I talked about cousins and aunts and the latest family drama.

When the discussions evolved into more personal matters, Mom and I exchanged worried looks. It was apparent Dad intended to address some matters with Marcus.

"It's not right that you keep Sophia and the kids away from us, Marcus. She's our only daughter; they're our only grandchildren. All we're asking is that you allow them to come see us more often."

My shoulders tensed. I held my breath, afraid of what might happen next.

Marcus stared my father down. "I would think you'd be grateful we're here now rather than complaining about the times we're not."

I could tell Dad's patience was waning. He was trying hard to control his frustration.

"Of course, we're glad you're here. But one measly visit a year doesn't cut it. It's not enough, Marcus. We want to see them more, and we'll do whatever it takes to make that happen."

"You're sounding a little too sure of yourself, old man. Sophia and the children belong to me, and they'll do as I say. They'll visit when I give them the okay to do so and not a moment more."

My father's jaw stiffened; the veins in his neck bulged. Marcus, on the other hand, remained calm and poised. Why shouldn't he? He held the upper hand. Every ounce of control belonged to him.

Without so much as a glance, he smirked as he spoke. "Sophia, collect the children and go to the car."

"But we've only just begun to eat." Hurt filled my mother's voice. I leaned in and hugged her, wishing I could stay in her embrace forever.

"It's okay, Mom. I promise, everything will be okay." Kissing her forehead, I took the children's hands in my own and started for the door.

My mother pleaded, "Sophia, please don't go. Oh, Marcus, please—please stay a while longer."

Now Marcus was losing his patience. "Sophia, to the car now!"

And just like that, the long-awaited visit with my parents came to an abrupt halt. And along with it, any hope I had of maintaining a relationship with them.

Oh, Sophia! How could you have been so naïve, so willing to conform to his demands, so easily fooled into giving up those who loved you most?

* * *

As I watched my children in quiet play, my mind slipped farther back in time. I thought about our courtship. *Had what I initially perceived as love and concern been nothing more than a ploy to control me? Had that been his plan all along?*

When we first met, the stigma of a high school pregnancy had taken up residence in my heart. I had studied hard and finished well, graduating with honors.

After taking off only one semester, I had jumped right into college—all while caring for my baby.

But regardless of how much I accomplished, it never seemed enough. Part of me still felt as if I had something to prove—to my parents, to my friends, even to my former church leaders. Though most were gracious toward me, I could sense the disappointment hiding behind their pained expressions. Perhaps if I acquired sufficient success, it would give them something to remember besides my teenage pregnancy.

Maybe that's why I fell so quickly for Marcus. He made me feel as if I had nothing to prove, at least in the beginning.

I had wandered into the coffee shop on campus in hopes of finding an empty table where I might sit and study. And there he stood, leaning against the counter, chatting with the barista about his drink order. In a rare moment of boldness, I discarded my study plan and made my way to the counter, intent on being noticed. That move is one of many I have lived to regret.

"Well, hello, pretty lady. I haven't seen you around, and I'm quite certain I would remember if I had." His wink entranced me as his eyes scanned me up and down. He didn't bother hiding it; he was pleased with my figure.

"Yes, I'm a new student. A freshman." Blushing, I silently reprimanded myself for sounding so much like one. *Why must I always say such awkward things when I'm nervous?*

"Well, you're the prettiest freshman I've seen in a long while. How about I buy you a coffee?"

"That'd be sweet. Thank you."

He placed his hand on my back and led me to a corner table for two. The table was occupied by a young man I recognized from my freshman Comp class. He sat by himself, the table littered with several open books.

As we approached, he stared at us with eyes voicing what his lips did not. "Uh, hello?"

"Excuse me, but we have need of this table. I'm sure you can find another more suitable location to complete your studies. Somewhere like your dorm room or, perhaps the library? It is always a good option." Marcus grinned at me and winked again.

The boy hesitated before shutting the open books and sliding them into his backpack. His eyes no longer posed questions. Instead, they exposed a subtle hint of some deeper emotion. Perhaps it was embarrassment? Disbelief? Maybe a touch of discouragement? I quickly set aside my concern, feeling only a tinge of pity for him as he walked away. *Little did I know one day Marcus would impose these same feelings of worthlessness on me.*

"Won't you take the seat of honor, my lady?" Marcus smiled as he held the chair for me.

"Why, thank you."

The casual conversation exchanged that first day led to deeper conversations in the days and weeks that followed. And true to my character, it didn't take long for our relationship to evolve into the sharing of more than conversation. I'm ashamed at how quickly I handed my heart over to him. *Had I not learned anything from my choices in high school?*

My mom tried to convince me the rumors weren't true, but her judgment was clouded. I wasn't a good girl after all. In her kind yet persistent way, she urged me to pursue God's best for my life. Mom's words graced my ears often enough to assure me my lifestyle did not match up, but I didn't care. There was something about Marcus that kept me coming back, something about him that kept me holding on, something that depleted every ounce of strength needed to resist him.

Truth be told, I simply wanted to be with him—no matter what that meant, no matter where that landed me. I could blame my ignorance on his handsome features. His dark complexion, jet black hair, and deep brown eyes baited me. His charm reeled me in. But his ability to make me feel like a princess—that is what set the hook, and once that hook was set, there was no breaking free.

Without a second thought, I jumped at his suggestion to quit college and marry him. Out of all the beautiful, perfect girls he could have chosen, he chose me! Absolutely elated, nothing could keep me from him and the beautiful life he'd promised. *What else could a girl like me hope to find in the man of her dreams?*

It didn't matter that he had never warmed up to Clara, only a baby at the time. I felt certain she would win him over. She won everyone over with her sweet smile and budding personality. Why would he be any different? It would simply take time. But I was wrong. *I've been wrong about so many things.*

With regret weighing heavy on my mind, I bathed my children, planted gentle kisses on their foreheads, and tucked them into bed. In the time it took to reach the cold cup of coffee awaiting me in the kitchen, he was home. The jingling of keys making their way into the lock stopped me in my tracks.

I held my breath as the front door swung open a few feet from me. He walked past, luggage in hand, without so much as a glance. *Had he even noticed me?* His features, tired and worn, replaced the anger and frustration ordinarily displayed on his hard face.

Without a word, he slipped into his office and closed the door. I could hear drawers snapping open and shut. Papers rustling. His chair squeaking each time he repositioned himself as if he were incapable of sitting still for any length of time.

The presence of such activity placed me on high alert. I had never heard such movement coming from his study. Normally, nothing but silence comes from that room other than an occasional cough or throat clearing. On even fewer occasions, snippets of muffled telephone conversations might be heard.

But days away from home followed by this ongoing busy-ness—and at this hour of the night—caused me great concern. *Could he tell I had been in there? Had I left something out of place in my rush to get back to the children? Had my fogginess caused me to overlook some tiny detail?* If so, I could not fathom the wrath that would soon be unleashed on me.

I removed my sandals and tiptoed down the hallway, barely breathing until I had traveled some distance past his office door. Staying close to the children would be necessary tonight. Retrieving a pillow and blanket from a nearby linen closet, I made myself a pallet outside Clara and Roger's bedroom door. Sleep would not be an option tonight; but fending it off would prove difficult. *Sophia, you must remain awake and alert—just in case.*

Not trusting myself to fully lie down, I propped my upper body against the wall. The night sky cast shadows on the wall adjacent to me. I hoped the lack of lamplight would hide my silhouette should he exit his office and look this way.

As I sat in the eerie, dark silence of my own home contemplating the fate of my children and myself, I felt certain of three things. One, something was definitely amiss. Two, that something involved my children and me. And three, a long, restless night was ahead. What

I didn't know was what to expect with the rising of the sun. *God, help me. This time, I'm really scared.*

CHAPTER 4

A Nightmare Revealed

I fought hard, but finally succumbed to sleep. Either Marcus hadn't concerned himself with why I was sleeping in the hallway, or he had simply failed to notice. Based upon his peculiar behavior when he arrived home last night, I couldn't be certain of either.

My sleep must have been fitful. I felt as unrested now as I had before falling asleep. I gathered my make-shift bed, rolled up the blanket, and tossed both blanket and pillow into the closet without care.

The children were beginning to stir when I peeked in at them. Sleepy eyes squinted opened and then closed again. *Such beautiful children. Oh, how I wish I could make everything all right for them.* "Good morning, my loves."

"Morning, Mommy." Clara yawned, stretching her arms high into the air and then rolling back to her side.

I sat on the edge of Roger's bed, pulling him near, blanket and all. The full weight of his small body nestled comfortably in my arms. I tickled him under the chin, trying to ease him into the morning. "Good morning, my sweet boy."

Rubbing both eyes with his tiny fists, he began to wiggle about until he was finally awake enough to sit up and look around. I expected him to nurse as he did each morning. But after only a moment, he lost interest and moved on to the box of toys he had abandoned at bedtime. I pulled at one of his dark curls; he didn't seem to notice. *I suppose my little guy is growing up whether I'm ready or not.*

After nudging Clara from her bed, I helped her choose her clothes for the day. She decided on a pale pink sweater and black leggings, always a favorite. Pulling Roger's clothes from the dresser, I picked him up and wrestled them on him. As soon as I gave him the clear, he darted full speed back to his toys and to whatever imaginary game I had interrupted moments before.

Clara settled into the corner near her dollhouse, attempting to change her favorite doll from its nightgown into an outfit closely resembling her own. I pulled Roger's wooden blocks from an upper shelf and placed them in the center of the room. Hopefully, between the toys and blocks, he'd have enough to keep him entertained until I returned.

"Clara, can you keep an eye on Roger while I go make breakfast for Daddy?" Her eyes darted toward the door. *Yes, baby girl. He's home.* She gave me a knowing glance and went back to dressing her doll.

Like Clara, I had no desire to encounter Marcus. But I'd rather be aware of his whereabouts than surprised by them. That's how I happened upon the private conversation unfolding on the other side of his office door. *Who was in there with him, and what did their presence mean for me and the children?*

***

I stood motionless on the outer side of the closed door. The voices reverberating inside chilled my spine. I could tell right away this was not a conversation I should be hearing, nor was it one I wanted to hear. Yet I remained at the door, ignoring the inner warnings signaling me to move on. I must listen a moment longer. Ear pressed lightly against the door's surface, I sought to better understand the mystery ahead.

I recognized only one of the voices. It belonged to Marcus's longtime friend and business partner, William Moss. Friends long before I came into the picture, Marcus and William had always been inseparable.

I had a sneaking suspicion William had never cared for me. At first it bothered me, but I soon grew accustomed to his snide remarks and less-than-amiable behavior toward me. In all honesty, I felt the same about him. I have often wondered what Marcus would be like if William hadn't been such an integral part of his life. *Would Marcus act any differently? Would he show more kindness to others? Would he demonstrate more love toward us?* I suppose none of that mattered now.

"I'm concerned for you, Marcus. Otherwise, I would never suggest such an arrangement. I've been your friend longer than I've been your business partner. Remember, I was there when you first came up with the notion of marrying Sophia. I hate to say it, but I warned you. Even then, I could tell that child of hers would cause nothing but trouble between the two of you. And if that wasn't enough, she went on and had a second one. I knew then, my friend, the day would come when this lifestyle would no longer suit you. I believe that day has arrived."

I pictured William shaking his head in disgust as he spoke these hateful words against the children and me. Something deep within me wanted to bust the door down and give him a piece of my mind. But I knew better.

"I can't argue with that, William. No doubt these children have caused me a great deal more stress than I'd bargained for, but I don't know. How can I be sure this plan is foolproof? How can I be sure this won't backfire on me?"

"Mr. Gadson, may I speak for a moment? Your partner and I go way back. Let's just say we've completed our fair share of business dealings through the years, many of which have been quite profitable to you, I might add. My team is professional. We operate by code only. No paper trails. No possible way to link you or your business to anything. We are that good. Because we're that good, we deal only with the most elite clientele. And believe me when I say they are more than willing to pay top dollar for the services we render. Should you decide to move forward, you will not be disappointed."

Marcus hesitated before speaking again. I envisioned him pausing as he often did when in deep thought – head tilted upward, eyes staring blankly at the ceiling, right hand rubbing his bearded chin. He spoke with a hint of conviction as if truly considering the innocence of the children, if only for a moment.

"While it's true these children have placed a tremendous strain on my marriage, I am not inclined to harm them per se. They are children after all. Tell me, Mr. ——"

"Johnson."

"Mr. Johnson, what options are available that would rid me of their incessant presence without causing unnecessary harm to befall them? Are there any such options? And if so, are there any guarantees these arrangements would be properly adhered to?"

"Well, it appears your business partner does know you well, Mr. Gadson. William took the liberty of selecting what he considered to be prime placements for each child. I'll allow him to share those selections with you."

"William–"

"Thank you, Mr. Johnson."

"Marcus, my friend, I believe you'll be happy with these selections. I propose that the children be placed in separate homes several hundred miles apart. This will alleviate the risk of them stumbling upon one another in years to come."

"And the details?"

"Of course. Clara's new home will be with an elderly widow. This widow has requested a child young enough, yet mature enough, to be groomed in the proper method of housekeeping and hospitality. Now I must tell you, the girl may be expected to provide entertainment on occasion. The widow didn't disclose what that would entail, but I'm inclined to think on the positive side. At any rate, the bulk of her service will be within the realm of housekeeping—a live-in slave of sorts.

The current housekeeper will spend the next few years training Clara to meet the widow's specific needs, as well as tutoring her in the basics of elementary education. Such training will ensure she gains the necessary knowledge to complete her requirements. I would say that makes her one lucky girl, but I won't mislead you. This widow is firm. She will not put up with childish ways, nor will she hesitate to discipline the girl should she fail to properly attend to her duties. As long as Clara abides by the rules and does things according to the old lady's standards, I'm sure they'll get along just fine. If the girl is half as compliant as her mother, this shouldn't be an issue."

"I see. And Roger?"

"Since Roger is your own flesh and blood, I knew his placement would be of greater concern to you. It took some time, but I believe I've found the perfect arrangement for the boy. Should you agree, he'll be placed in the home of a wealthy, middle-aged couple who have been unable—even after several attempts, I'm told—to bear a son. His purpose will be to carry on the family name and, someday, take over the family business."

"I see. Neither sounds all that disturbing to me. What about the logistics of this?"

"New birth certificates will be drawn up for each child. They'll be equipped with fictitious names, birthplaces, et cetera. Every 't' will be crossed, every 'i' dotted. Appearing authentic in every way."

"Hmmm, it's certainly worth considering. How soon could these arrangements be made?"

"As soon as you give the word. But may I encourage you to make a decision soon? The availability of these *softer* homes cannot be guaranteed for long. They are not near as easy to come by as the typical, shall we say, less friendly placements."

"And may I remind you, Marcus, pursuing this opportunity is imperative for the success of our business. Without the profits from this deal, we are all but sunk."

"I don't need to be reminded of this, William. I am fully aware of the state of our affairs."

"Now, Mr. Johnson, what about my wife? You suggested there may be opportunities for her to also earn her keep? Mind you, I'm not keen on sharing my wife's attention—thus, this whole discussion about the children. However, if she proves to be less than attentive to my needs once the children are gone, then I'll have no need of her."

"I understand."

"Very well. Put together a proposal for me. One for the children only. One to include Sophia. Use your code language, of course. I'm sure William can educate me on the deciphering of it. I'll make a final decision once those are reviewed."

I stood in stunned silence, feet all but frozen to the floor. *Move, Sophia! Move! You've got to get away from this door!*

CHAPTER 5

Borrowed Time

Breathing deeply, I moved one foot forward and then the other. I wanted so badly to grab the children and make a run for it, but I had no place to run. Even if I had, I could never outrun the nagging words I'd heard spoken in my own home. *Could he really do such a thing?*

My heart tried to convince me Marcus was incapable of that degree of evil. Perhaps this was all a grave misunderstanding. Maybe the words I thought I heard were not his words at all. *Could I somehow be mistaken?* Though my heart fought against it, my mind knew the truth. And the truth was not pretty.

My life was in danger. Even worse, if his plan was carried out, the lives of my children would be at great risk. Uprooted. Taken to unknown places to live among unknown people. Strangers who would care little to nothing about their well-being. My heart filled with trepidation; I had walked straight into a nightmare. I only hoped I could survive with my life—and the lives of my children—intact.

As much as I feared staying, I knew this was not the time to run. Though there would never be a fail-safe plan, an escape of this magnitude couldn't be carried out without some strategizing. *But where would I even begin?*

I decided it best to stick to my normal routine as much as possible. The last thing I wanted was for Marcus to become suspicious. Making my way into the kitchen, I began the task of preparing breakfast, struggling to carry on as if everything were okay. *Lord, please help me pull this off.*

I whipped up a skillet of cheesy scrambled eggs to serve with the biscuits I had prepared earlier in the week. I then made a large batch of sausage gravy in case Marcus invited his guests to breakfast. While having guests at mealtime was not a common occurrence in our home, I found it best to be prepared for anything.

After placing breakfast on the warmer, I pulled several small oranges from the fruit bowl and peeled them. I forced the oranges, two at a time, into the electric juicer and allowed it to do its magic. The juice looked and smelled delightful, but the children and I wouldn't dare drink it. The less we aggravated Marcus, the easier it was to live with him.

Before long, the squeaky office door told me their meeting had ended. My chest began to pound as Marcus and his guests sauntered toward the kitchen. I stepped to the far side of the room, hoping they wouldn't notice me as they passed the open doorway. But I didn't move quickly enough.

I rubbed my hands on my apron as if to press out any wrinkles that may have formed since last wearing it. Glancing up as the men entered the kitchen, my eyes settled on the face of the unfamiliar man. His smile caught me off guard. It wasn't meant to be friendly or to put me at ease. It was the type of smile that told me he knew of things I did not. My eyes fell to the floor. My insides shivered.

"Sophia, I hope you've prepared enough breakfast to feed these kind men."

Somehow, I managed to speak. "Yes, of course. There should be more than enough." I pulled the finest table settings from the cupboard and placed one for each of them at the table. Carefully, I removed the eggs, biscuits and gravy from the warmer and placed each in the center of the table near the jars of jelly and jam I always kept on hand.

Finding my voice again, I asked, "Would any of you care for a glass of freshly-squeezed orange juice?"

"I prefer coffee; make it black." William was fond of ordering me around.

"Orange juice will do just fine," said the unfamiliar man who, undoubtedly, enjoyed this game of making me uncomfortable.

Marcus said nothing but observed my every move as I served both men the drinks they requested. After pouring Marcus his glass of orange juice, I moved slowly about the kitchen. I wiped down the already spotless countertops with a damp cloth, then busied myself by tidying up the dishtowel drawer. My mind, littered with fear and indecisiveness, considered my next move. *Should I stay put? Should I slip out?* Marcus broke the silence. "Run along now, Sophia. Your services are no longer needed. At least not for the time being." All three men chuckled as I excused myself. His last words hanging over me like a dark cloud.

"*... at least not for the time being.*"

I shuddered to think what might be required of me if escape failed to come soon.

* * *

By the time the kitchen cleared of the three men, the children were hungry for their breakfast. I strapped Roger into his highchair and spooned leftover eggs and pieces of biscuit onto his plate. He picked them up by handfuls, shoveling them into his mouth as if he had not eaten for days.

"Slow down, little man." He flashed me a grin and reached for more. *Goodness, he really is hungry.*

I tried to sound cheerful for the children, but judging by Clara's demeanor, my attempts were not convincing. I studied her a moment longer. Though she held a spoon in her hand and appeared to be eating, her mind had traveled somewhere far away. I watched her move eggs by the spoonful from one side of the plate to the other. Had I not been paying attention I may have been fooled into thinking she had eaten more than she had.

"Clara, honey, you must eat more than just a couple of bites."

"But Mommy, I'm not hungry today."

I frowned as I looked at her half-eaten sausage patty. "Two more bites."

Staring at me blankly, she went through the motions. One tiny bite, then another; somehow, she knew I had no fight left in me. Her nibbling would have to do until lunch time. I'd just have to make sure she ate enough then to make up for what she refused to eat now.

I wiped Roger's face and scrubbed his fingers clean before sending the two of them into the living area to play. Marcus had retreated to his office shortly after the men left. I hoped he would stay there long enough for me to attend to some business of my own: the business of plotting our escape.

* * *

The house was quiet the next couple of days. It was almost too quiet. This lack of activity created ample time for my mind to run away with every possible "what-if" scenario.

What if he sneaks the children away while I'm sleeping? What if the black limousine shows up and leaves with my children? How would I ever live without them? How would they ever make it without me?

I dumped a basket of clean clothes onto the couch and began sorting them into four separate stacks, one for each of us. As I sorted, I gazed at the children. Both were curled up on the ottoman, sharing an oversized blanket and fluffy pillow. The television showcased scenes from their favorite afternoon cartoon. Both sets of eyes glued on it as if they hadn't already seen it numerous times.

Clearing a spot on the couch, I sank into it and pulled the nearest pile of clothes toward me. One of Roger's tiny socks caught my eye. Such a small, insignificant item by itself. *Much like me*, I thought. Rummaging through the stack, I reunite it with its mate. Pausing before setting them down, it occurs to me–Separate, they accomplish little. But together, they find their purpose. *Had I expected to find my purpose by marrying Marcus? Had I been that one lone sock, unable to function on my own? Did that description still fit me?*

I sighed, inhaling a big breath and then blowing it out until my cheeks fully deflated. If only these disturbing thoughts – and the immense fear I sensed welling up inside–could be exhaled as easily.

With Roger's clothes folded, I moved on to Clara's. *What can I do to get us out of this house before Marcus notices our absence?*

Sneaking away in the car would be the most logical choice, if it weren't for Marcus keeping such a tight grip on the keys. I'm embarrassed at how easily he convinced me to give up my car. I should have recognized his antics. I should have known I couldn't trust him to allow me the use of his car as promised. But I fell for it, same as always. Without my car, or the keys to his, the children and I weren't going anywhere. And that's exactly how he wanted it.

When Marcus first mentioned the idea of one car, it seemed reasonable. I seldom left the house anyway, except for quick trips to the grocery store or routine doctor appointments. I never suspected giving up my car would be the catalyst to losing my freedom. It served as the first phase in a two-step process. He did away with my car. Then, he began to eliminate my need to leave the house.

He arranged for our groceries to be ordered online and delivered to our front porch. This seemed ideal at first. I mean, wow! Buying groceries without leaving your home? That's genius! But it's not such a grand idea when it causes you to become imprisoned in your own home.

He demanded that trips to the doctor be made in only extreme circumstances. Since our exposure to others had been limited, the children and I were rarely sick. Because we seldom experienced illness, this also worked to his advantage.

To top it all off, he contacted the school district to ensure our home would be added to the bus route when Clara begins kindergarten. I had always dreamed of driving my children to school, of being one of those moms who baked cookies and chaperoned field trips and whatever else homeroom moms do. But this dream, like so many others, will likely not come to fruition. All because I couldn't think for myself. What a great price I'm paying for that now. I can't help but wonder how much more it will cost me in the end.

Whether we leave or stay, Marcus will do everything in his power to have the final say and that terrifies me. Even if we escape this house, will it be possible to ever fully escape his reach?

CHAPTER 6

Sandwiches and Secrecy

I shifted my attention from the laundry I had been folding to the home in which I had been living. Though an older home, I had fallen in love with the charm of it. Its two-story frame resembled a dollhouse my father had gifted to me on my eighth birthday. The dollhouse had afforded me many hours of childhood fun. Perhaps that's why I agreed to move into this house so quickly; it reminded me of happier times.

When we first moved in, the children and I spent many afternoons playing at the edge of the woods. We especially enjoyed exploring the trails closest to the house. Though curious about the full thirty acres, I couldn't gather enough bravery to venture farther out. Fearing Marcus would grow angry should he step outside and find us absent, we stayed within view of the house at all times.

As I reflected on the past, the truth became more and more apparent. I had allowed myself to be isolated, little by little, until the outside world and everyone in it seemed only a figment of my imagination.

How did I ever fall for this? Why did I not speak up? Why had I trusted him so much? I forced away these hard questions and the underlying insult they threw at my intelligence. This was no time to weigh myself down with more guilt.

One cartoon ended and another began as I stood to my feet. I didn't bother turning off the television or suggesting that the children go play. A few more moments of quiet would do us all good.

I put away the laundry while continuing to toss around one silent idea after another.

We could probably sneak out during the night and make our way down the driveway without much difficulty. The partially downed fence near the gate should give us an easy way out. *But then what?*

We could use the pretense of going for a walk on the trail, and just not come back. We could follow the trail as far as it would take us and then venture into the woods. *Could we make it to a neighbor's house before nightfall?* Oh, how I prayed spending the night in the dark woods with my children would not be necessary. *Could we make it somewhere safe before Marcus could catch up with us?*

Whatever the plan, it would be best carried out when Marcus leaves town again. But which route should we choose? *Would the woods or the roadway be safest? Could either be considered safe?* There was no way to be sure.

Though the plan lacked clarity, one thing was certain. We had to be ready when the opportunity presented itself. We must be prepared to leave with only a moment's notice. It was time to exercise initiative while also proceeding with caution. It was time to ready ourselves for escape.

I tried to organize my thoughts without paper, fearing handwritten notes would create an unnecessary risk. We would need warm clothing, thick jackets, perhaps a small blanket or two to combat the chilly early spring nights. A couple of flashlights. Walking shoes. Enough water and snacks for a few days, though I prayed it wouldn't take nearly that long.

I might be able to prepare extra peanut butter and jelly sandwiches while making lunch today. *What else might we need? Think, Sophia, think.*

I entered the kitchen and began pulling our lunch staples together with a purpose like never before. Peanut butter. Jelly. White bread. On second thought, maybe I should substitute syrup for the jelly since refrigerating the sandwiches would not be an option.

My hands, grasping a plastic butter knife, spread the smooth mixture over each slice of bread. One sandwich for me. One for Clara. One-half for Roger. Without thinking, I trimmed the crust from each one – a habit carried over from my own childhood.

The entrance to Marcus's office could not be seen from my position in the kitchen. Since I lacked this visual, my ears sought out any sounds indicative of trouble. Confident all was clear, I crammed the peanut butter and syrup sandwiches into individual bags and sealed them tightly. With a flick of my wrist, I tossed the bags into the nearest cabinet, hiding them behind a box of trash liners. Leaning over the countertop for support, I released a shaky breath before moving on to the second batch.

Peanut butter. Syrup. White bread. One for me. One for Clara. One-half for Roger. But this time I didn't trim the crust. We might need it.

I paused before retrieving more sandwich bags and repeating the process. With three extra portions readied and hidden out of sight, my focus shifted to today's lunch preparations.

Fresh pita bread, smoked turkey and pepper jack cheese – all Marcus's favorites–called to me from the refrigerator. I refused them. *What if Marcus joined us for lunch? What if he noticed I had opened his personal stash?* It simply wasn't worth the fight.

Instead, I prepared traditional peanut butter and grape jelly sandwiches for the children and me. Adding sliced grapes and mandarin oranges on the side helped to break up the redundancy of it all.

"Clara, honey, come join me at the table."

Without being told, Roger followed close behind his big sister. Connecting with my children at meal-time has always been a priority of mine, but today it felt anything but natural. I struggled to string together words that would put my children at ease. *How could I do so when I felt so anxious myself? How could I comfort them when I couldn't wrangle my own troubled thoughts into submission?* Instead, we ate our lunch in silence.

Clara understood this increasingly familiar mood. Roger was too young or too tired to care, falling asleep in his chair before he cleared his plate. Though it still didn't equate to her normal helping, Clara had eaten more for lunch than at breakfast. For this, I felt thankful.

"Mommy, may I be excused now? I ate all my fruit and some of my sandwich."

"Yes, Clara. Go quietly to your room. I'll bring Roger in shortly."

She scooted her chair from the table and walked to her room in silence. Moments later I placed one hand under Roger's bottom, the other behind his head, and prayed he would stay asleep as I lifted him from his chair. Evidence of peanut butter lay in smudges at the corners of his lips; I didn't bother to wipe them away. Peanut butter on the sheets was the least of my concerns today.

I nudged the bedroom door open with my elbow, surprised to find Clara already sleeping. A different fear crept into my heart. This behavior was unusual for her. *Could she be sick?*

I placed Roger into his bed. Unaware in his sleepy state, he grabbed his favorite teddy bear and pulled it close. After covering him with his bedspread, I moved across the room to Clara's bed. Her head was cool to the touch. *Good, no fever.* But if she's not sick, what could be causing this odd behavior? Could it be sadness stealing my sweet Clara from me? Has she fallen into depression? Is that even possible for children her age? Even as worry clung to my heart, resolution settled within me. The process of filling our backpacks had now become of utmost importance.

* * *

It took a full three days of squandering a moment here and there, but I had managed to pack both mine and Clara's largest backpacks with the essentials. I continued to tally the list of items we might need.

By doing so, I had come up with a couple of things I had not considered before. Extra batteries for the flashlights. An old compass Marcus had discarded some time ago. I had found it in the children's toy box while straightening their rooms before bed last night. I can only hope it'll work well enough to lead us from this prison to a place of safety.

My stomach felt queasy when I thought of what it might take to arrive at such a place. *Does that place even exist for us? And if so, will we find it? And if we somehow manage to find it, how will we know we've arrived?*

With so many unknowns dangling before me, one certainty held true: if my plans fail to take flight, we will never have another opportunity to fly. Marcus will make sure of that.

CHAPTER 7

Boots and Backpacks

At the sound of the black limousine coming up the drive, Marcus emerged from his office, overnight bag in hand. He walked out the door without a word. It was all so unusual.

The past few days he had entered the kitchen only to retrieve his dinner and carry it into his office. He hadn't concerned himself with returning the dirty dishes to the kitchen. This was something he always handled himself to keep me—and any unnecessary clutter—from invading his office. And now he leaves with nothing but an overnight bag? One he never ordered me to pack? *What in the world was going on here?*

I assumed he would not be gone long, having carried such a small bag with him. Would he be gone overnight as it suggested, or was he using it as a briefcase, intending to return home within an hour or two?

What am I to do? My thoughts wrestled within me. *What if this was our last chance to make a run for it? What if the next men through that gate were the ones summoned to take my children away?*

I simply couldn't chance that happening.

I ran down the hall, grabbing our backpacks from their usual spot on the coat rack. They were filled with everything, except the sandwiches. I'd worried about hiding our supplies in plain view, but worried more that he'd notice if I'd moved them out of sight.

After gathering the sandwiches from the kitchen cabinet, I sprinted down the hall toward the children's room. Before opening the door, I forced myself to pause so as not to frighten them. *Breathe, Sophia, breathe.* Turning the knob, I entered as casually as my anxiousness would permit.

"Clara, how about we go for a little walk down the trail?"

Her eyes lit up. "Really, Mom? We haven't done that in forever!"

"Yes, sweetie. But if we're going, we must go quickly. Run and use the bathroom, then put your boots on. I'll grab your coat."

"Okay, Mommy. Roger, we're going on the trail!" Her excitement over this unexpected outing almost made me feel guilty.

In the time it took Clara to use the bathroom and get her boots on, I had Roger dressed and ready. Pulling coats from the rack, I wasted no time putting them on the children while walking toward the terrace.

We made our way down the stairs, across the yard, and onto the nearest trail. All the while, looking over my shoulder to be sure there were no signs of Marcus or the black limousine.

Our pace on the trail proved much slower than I had envisioned. *At this rate, would we ever make it out of these woods?* I picked up Roger. He was small for his age, but still wouldn't be an easy load to carry. *Surely, I can at least carry him to the end of the trail.*

We had no time for piddling. We needed to cover as much ground as possible while daylight remained on our side. The less time on the trail, the more time to navigate the woods before darkness took over.

It didn't take the children long to realize this was not a leisurely stroll. There would be little time to investigate ants crawling over logs or to capture a passing toad. This walk would be more work than play, and they weren't at all happy about it.

Clara began asking questions. Roger grew whinier with each step. I tried to hide my frustration and keep my tears at bay, but I wasn't doing a good job at either.

"Clara, honey, I know you don't understand but—"

"We're hiding from Daddy?"

Stunned silence stood between us. *What could I say to help her understand without terrifying her in the process?*

"Oh, sweet girl. I'm so sorry you and Roger are caught in the middle of this … yes, we are hiding from Daddy. It's not good for us to be with him right now. It is time for us to get away, to find someplace better for us."

"Someplace where Daddy won't hit you, Mommy? Someplace where Daddy won't scare us?"

"Yes, Clara. A place like that."

"Are we almost there, Mommy? Are we almost to the better place?"

I sighed louder than I meant to and forced a smile. "We're closer than we were a little while ago. But, Clara, it's important that we keep moving. And that we walk as quickly as we can. It won't be easy, especially with your little brother. But it's crucial that we not stop any more than necessary. Can you help me do that?"

"Yes, Mommy. I'll help you. Even if my legs get tired. I'll keep walking."

"My sweet, sweet Clara, how did I get so lucky to have you as my girl?"

She smiled, took Roger by the hand and coaxed him into running after a butterfly that had already circled us a time or two. I walked quickly to keep up and enjoyed the momentary giggles of my children as they pursued the butterfly.

Had God sent this beautiful butterfly to distract my children? Or could it be a message intended solely for me? Stories I had heard as a child danced through my mind, keeping rhythm with the butterfly fluttering above my children.

I smiled as I thought about the old white bus that stopped in my neighborhood, week in and week out. It carried me and about a dozen other children to the

Wednesday night services at a local church. We would eat a hot meal, play a few games, and listen to stories about God's love for us. And if we worked hard enough through the week—or crammed well enough during the bus ride—to recite that week's bible verse, we received a special treat.

My parents didn't attend church at the time. In fact, it would be many years before they settled into the rhythm of regular church attendance. Dad simply couldn't see the benefit of giving up his Sundays at home.

Though they didn't attend themselves, they were never opposed to me going. Not only that, but mom's study helps earned me a weekly treasure more than once. Between her encouragement and my own determination, there was seldom a week that passed without me rummaging through the beloved treasure box. Carrying home one of the many delights found within was often the highlight of my week. Funny how I never realized the real treasure was hidden within the verses themselves, not in a box of tiny trinkets. *How had I missed that revelation all these years?*

I tried to recall the last time I rode that bus. *Had I made a conscious decision to not go back to church? Had I grown tired of it? Had I become too busy?* I think more than anything, I felt convinced I had outgrown my need of it. Only a handful of adults in my life showed any interest in attending; even fewer friends considered it worthwhile—and all of them seemed to be getting along just fine.

By skipping out on the mid-week bus ride, I had unknowingly set in motion a series of goodbyes, paving the way for one poor decision after another. When I said goodbye to church, I also left behind those people who had worked so hard at helping me understand my value. Maybe worst of all, I left behind that little girl who desperately needed those influences in her life.

Where had that girl gone? The girl who found it easy to believe she was loved. By her parents. By the people at that church. By the God of the universe. *Why had I pushed her away? Oh, how I wish I could find her!*

A faint humming noise brought me back to the present. I snapped my fingers; the children clambered to my side, butterfly forgotten. I resolved to block out the sounds of nature, honing in on that one sound that didn't belong.

My heart dropped. It was the limousine. We must not be far from the main road which meant the limousine must be only moments from our home. Marcus would arrive soon, and we were still close enough to be found should he venture this direction.

Clara and I locked eyes.

"Which way do we go, Mommy?"

Panic set in. I couldn't think.

"Mommy! Which way do we go?"

I suddenly remembered the old compass I had stuffed in the side pocket of my backpack. *Why hadn't I been relying on it this whole time?* I held it upright and found that we were heading east. My best guess was that the nearest neighbor would be to our north.

"This way, Clara!"

I scooped Roger into my arms despite the protest of my aching muscles.

"No, Mommy! I want to walk!"

"Not now, Roger!"

I'm not sure if it was the sternness in my voice or the panic in my eyes, but he submitted to me carrying him without further objection. I held the compass tight as if it were a life source. At the moment, it seemed to be our only one.

* * *

A little over an hour had passed since Roger had fallen asleep in my arms. Feeling as if both arms might break off at any moment, I continued to push myself; sheer adrenaline kept me moving.

Clara and I kept walking until the darkness became so black even our flashlights were of little help. When we could no longer maneuver safely, I had to call it a night.

Leaning against the nearest tree, I slid my backpack onto the ground and sank into a sitting position. It felt good to stretch my legs, but even better to free my arms from the twenty-something pounds of sleeping child I'd been carrying.

Every ounce of energy had been expended; there was nothing left. Clara curled up beside me, too exhausted to worry about the chill in the air or the sounds of the night. I pulled my children closer, thankful for the small blankets I had forced into the backpacks.

As the children slept, I reassessed our situation. *We had escaped the house, but how had we not yet been found? Had Marcus searched the roadways instead? And now that we were forced to do what I had dreaded most, spending the night in the woods, how could I be sure we'd be okay? Would I be capable of leading my children out of these woods? Did I have the strength, the courage, the ability to keep them from whatever dangers we might encounter?*

Drowning in this impenetrable darkness, I felt anything but strong or brave or able. *Lord, won't you please keep us safe?*

* * *

The first hint of day broke through the treetops. Wincing, I untangled my body from my sleeping children, every muscle screaming in protest. Crawling toward a felled tree, I leaned against it and used it as a prop to lift myself. Glancing around, I wondered how far we had come.

I contemplated whether Marcus would gravitate toward the woods in search of us or assume we had taken to the road. I prayed the latter would be true. If he had chosen to check the woods, he might be upon us any moment. *What would I do then?*

It took only minimal persuasion to stir the children from their sleep.

"Good morning, my loves. Let's eat a bite before we head out."

Clara cleared away a section of leaves with her hand, creating a sort of makeshift table for the two of them. I unwrapped their sandwiches first, encouraging them to eat quickly so we could be on our way. Then I indulged myself; peanut butter never tasted so good.

Roger kept his eyes on me. "Mommy, can we go home now?"

"Not yet, sweetie."

"I don't like it here."

"I know, Roger." I ran my fingers through his hair. "But the woods hold so many wonderful adventures for a boy like you."

Unconvinced, he wrinkled his tiny nose in disapproval.

"Listen." I cupped my hand to my ear. "Do you hear the birds singing? I bet if we watch closely, we'll even see another squirrel or two."

"I see squirrels at home, Mommy."

"Yes, I suppose you do."

Clara rolled her eyes at her little brother, "Roger, we can't go home ever again. So, leave Mommy alone about it!"

Roger's eyes welled up with tears. I'm not sure which upset him more, the fact that Clara had raised her voice at him or that we wouldn't be going home.

I knew I should say something to reassure and comfort my children, but once again, the words would not come. Gathering our belongings, I clasped their small hands in my own. We began another trek through the woods. *Had I made a mistake bringing my children out here?*

* * *

All in all, the children were such good troupers. As long as I kept a cheerful tone to my voice, Roger seemed to buy into the idea that we were on an adventure. Though Clara knew better, she plodded along with few complaints. Her biggest goal seemed to be finding creative ways to satisfy Roger's curiosity. With child-like wonder, she drew his attention to the wonders hidden in plain sight all around us.

She pointed to a nearby cluster of rocks, "Look, Roger—a lizard!"

Roger's short legs carried him with surprising speed, causing the small creature to scurry away. He giggled and ran after it until it escaped under a mound of leaves.

"Mommy, it's fast!"

"Yes, baby, it ran fast." He had no idea the lizard was running for its life, much like we were running for ours. *Oh, how I hoped we would be as successful at evading capture as that lizard.*

I checked the compass once more before returning it to my backpack.

"Come on, sweetie. Let's keep moving. Here, Mommy will carry you awhile."

Picking Roger up and placing him on my hip, we kept moving in the direction I hoped would lead us to freedom. Though I longed to gain as much ground as possible, the urgency I initially felt had given way to a slightly more relaxed pace. Maybe because the daylight offered a sense of new beginnings. Maybe because I now understood the limitations present when venturing through the woods with children. Or maybe the nagging presence of uncertainty was the force holding me back. *Where might these woods take us? How could I be sure Marcus wouldn't be lying in wait for us, wherever we ended up?*

These worries and more cluttered my mind, but we had no choice. We had to keep moving. We had to keep searching for someone willing to help. *Oh Lord, won't You please lead us to that someone? Won't You please lead us to help?*

CHAPTER 8

Cat and Mouse

"Sophia!" *Where could that woman be?* "Sophia!"

"Marcus, should I check the grounds? She couldn't have gone far."

"I suppose it wouldn't hurt, William. Perhaps she's taken the children for a walk on the trail. You check the grounds; I'll do another walk-through of the house to see if anything is out of place."

"Alright. I'm on it."

There is no way she would run off with the children. She's not that brave, nor is she smart enough, for that matter. There must be a logical explanation.

"Sophia, come out at once!"

Marcus rounded the corner and stood face to face with an empty coat rack.

"Well, well, well. What have we here?"

What is that woman up to? She and the children would have no need of backpacks or coats if they were simply playing outside or taking a short walk on the trail. Has she been snooping around? Has she somehow figured out my plan?

"There's no sign of them in the yard, Marcus, but I'm almost certain I heard voices off in the distance. It sounded as if it might be coming from deeper within the woods."

"Hmmm, isn't this an interesting turn of events? It may be time for an unexpected walk in the woods, William."

"It certainly appears that way. Why don't we call Mr. Johnson? A third person may prove useful, especially if Sophia has elicited help from outsiders. Afterall, he's just as interested in their return as we are, maybe more so. He does have clients waiting."

"I'm not the least concerned with outside interference. I've gone to great lengths to alleviate any such possibilities. However, I'm not opposed to Mr. Johnson's assistance in retrieving them."

"I'll give him a call, Marcus, but I don't expect he'll make it here before dark."

"That's alright. We'll postpone our search until tomorrow morning. It'll do them good to spend the night in the woods. Sophia will be so frightened she'll be begging us to get them out of there before nightfall tomorrow."

"Very well. I'll return in the morning with Mr. Johnson. What do you think? Does eight a.m. sound okay to you?"

"Yes, William, that should work just fine."

* * *

Marcus locked the door behind William and proceeded to the kitchen for a cup of strong, black coffee. He expected to nab only a meager portion of sleep tonight anyway. His anger burned too deeply to allow anything more.

Did she really think she could pull this off? Did she assume I wouldn't figure out what she was doing? Stupid woman! She's done it this time. She only thought she had it rough before.

Pacing the floor, he mulled over the plan to be executed once William returned with Mr. Johnson. *Once the search begins, it shouldn't take long to locate Sophia and the children. Should I immediately apprehend them, or should I follow behind, toying with them? The latter would likely torment Sophia more. A nice game of hunt or be hunted—it does sound appealing.*

Coffee in hand, he scouted the house for additional clues but found none. Had Sophia concocted this plan to run away, or had she simply seized the opportunity to make a run for it? He was inclined to believe the latter, knowing she had a reputation for acting on impulse with scant regard for long-term consequences. Such behavior had always been her weakness. *And look where it's landed her now.* He shook his head in disapproval while gloating over the image of her cowering in the dark woodlands. *Serves her right.*

* * *

The doorbell rang at promptly eight o'clock. William and Mr. Johnson stood at full attention, eager to receive their assignments.

"Marcus, we are ready to set out."

"Very well. We'll begin on the trail and split off as needed from there. It shouldn't be difficult to track them down. She couldn't have gone far with two children in tow."

"Once apprehended, what are your intentions, Mr. Gadson?" Mr. Johnson saw no need for pleasantries. "Will you be ready to complete our transaction at that time?"

"With the children, yes. There will be no need to bring them back to the house. But I have some business to attend to with my wife before turning her over to you."

Yes, I'll have my time with Sophia before sending her off. She owes me that much. And when I tire of her, as I most surely will, then I'll complete the deal. One day, she'll look back and wish she had never crossed me.

"Very well, Mr. Gadson. I'll have my people on standby for the exchange."

"Gentlemen, let's move out, shall we? I am anxious to get this little game of mouse hunt underway." *Sophia, my darling, I'm coming for you.*

* * *

Marcus held his hand in the air to signal silence. Both William and Mr. Johnson stood frozen, awaiting their next instruction. Recognizing the faint voices of children in the distance, the three of them exchanged knowing glances.

The search had taken longer than anticipated, causing Marcus to question how Sophia and the children had covered so much ground in such a short amount of time. *Had she received outside help?* Either way, they were close and that's all that mattered at the moment.

The men spread out in three directions, making a half circle around the area they believed Sophia and the children to be hiding. Sophia's voice sounded stationary. She spoke to the children as if nothing out of the ordinary had occurred. *She was in for a big surprise.*

Marcus took small steps, purposely intending some to be heard. He wanted Sophia to know he was close. He wanted her to fear being captured. But first, he wanted her to fear being pursued. And he was prepared to feed that fear as long as necessary for an all-out panic to ensue. He felt confident the wait would not be long.

* * *

The morning air was damp—the sky, cloudy. The absence of sunlight gave the daytime woods an eerie feel, almost as if evening were already upon us.

"Mommy, I am done with my sandwich."

"Alright, sweetie. Let's pick up after ourselves. Clara, can you dump the breadcrumbs out and then stick the baggies in your backpack? We don't want to leave any trash lying around."

"Yes, ma'am."

As we readied ourselves to head out, I heard an unusual rustling of leaves to our left. I said nothing to the children but listened intently. *Could it be just wind filtering through the treetops?* I heard it a second time. This time it appeared to be localized more to the right of us. Fear rushed into my chest like water rushing from an open dam.

"Children, let's be on our way. Quickly, now."

Unsure of which way to go, instinct told me to move in the only direction I hadn't heard the noise. Straight ahead. This would get us somewhat off track, but it couldn't be helped. If Marcus was responsible for this noise on either side of us, I had no desire to walk straight into him. I would avoid him as long as possible.

Leading the children by the hand, we resumed our hike through the woods. This time at a quicker pace. My ears tuned in, seeking any hint of being followed. My eyes mimicked those of a soldier stationed on high alert, constantly surveying the surroundings for any sudden movement. Still, I spoke nothing of this to the children.

Before long, my suspicions were confirmed. There in the woods a shadow lurked, partly hidden behind a large oak tree. *He's here. He's found us. Oh God, what should we do? We can't outrun him. We can't evade him. Lord, we're trapped. Please send help.*

This prayer had barely escaped my lips when a thundering roar resounded a short distance from us. The otherwise serene woods now boomed loud and threatening. The children scrambled behind me. My eyes scanned the woods, trying to identify the source and precise location of the roar. *Was it coming toward us?*

Another roar broke the silence; a man's voice mingled with it, "Marcus, run!" I almost didn't recognize the panicked voice belonging to William.

I watched as two random figures merged with a third, all darting off in the direction opposite the children and me. The shadow of a fourth figure tagged behind them. I stood paralyzed. *Was that a bear? I had no idea bears lived in this area. Had the children and I really been wandering around in woods inhabited by bears?* The thought of it made my skin crawl.

"Shoot it! Shoot it!" The command belonged to Marcus. Gunfire billowed, pelting an extra measure of tension over the neighboring woodlands. Pushing my fear aside, another thought crossed my mind. This was our chance! I pulled Roger into my arms and held tight to Clara's hand. We ran with all our might, refusing to slack off until we could no longer hear man or bear.

CHAPTER 9

The Dark of Night

S lowing our pace, I combed the woods for a sufficient hiding place. No doubt Marcus would persist in his quest to capture us. He would not give up easily. A bear chase may slow him down, but it wouldn't deter him from carrying out his evil plan.

Pulling a lukewarm water bottle from my backpack, I gave each child a drink and then took a sip myself. Faint conversations traveling through invisible sound waves interrupted our rest. Our gate to freedom was narrowing.

I looked around, frantic to discover some form of reprieve. *What could we do? Where could we hide? Calm down, Sophia. Breathe, just breathe.*

It was then I noticed a rock formation jutting from the hillside a few hundred feet ahead of us. Vines and thick underbrush had grown tall and covered most of the rock's surface, making its visibility slim. *How had I even noticed this?–Thank you, God.*

Maybe we could hide under its cover, if only Roger would stay quiet long enough. I guided the children toward the rock, ducking into the shadows of the thicket along its edge. This area was already void of sunlight and getting darker by the moment. We crept along the wall and stumbled upon a slender opening. *Could it be an entryway?*

With arms extended, my hand rested on an old, rusty latch. I clung to it, applying pressure until it gave way. Forcing the door open, the children and I inched into a chilling darkness.

It seemed we had stumbled upon the remnants of an old root cellar—one clearly vacated some time ago. The thought of snakes lurking within made my stomach churn, but I had no choice. As dank, dirty and frigid as it proved to be, it remained our best option. This make-shift shelter must serve as a hideout, albeit temporary. Placing the children inside, I prayed these walls would shield them from any impending danger. *Lord, please protect them in ways I cannot.*

With little time to waste, I pressed my index finger to my lips, begging silence from my children. Stepping outside the hidden door, I secured it behind me as best I could. I purposely allowed the latch to dangle loosely, hoping to avoid unnecessary clatter.

Making my way back across the camouflaged ledge, I worked to keep my frame hidden behind the vines and thicket. Moving sure-footed and with great care I set out, intent on steering Marcus and his helpers away from my children. Circling the section of woods housing his position, I found myself standing opposite the place I had hidden them. *Lord, help them stay put – and quiet—long enough.*

Making enough noise to ensure I'd be heard, I made my move. I ran, hoping to be followed. I ran, fearing I'd be caught. My only goal was to draw Marcus and his men away from the cellar and the treasures hidden within— my two beautiful, brown-eyed children. Unprotected. Innocent. Helpless.

Lord, keep them safe. Guide my feet. Give me strength.

* * *

As the final evidence of daylight surrendered to a blanket of darkness, a deep-seated uneasiness enveloped me. These thick woods were difficult to navigate during the day; I could not imagine traipsing around in the black of night. But I could not stow away until morning; I must make my way back to the children. They could not remain alone in that cellar overnight.

But before retracing my steps, I must avert the enemy. A lump caught in my throat. *How long had I viewed my husband as an enemy?* A deep sadness intertwined my fear. Ignoring both, I forced myself to refocus on the task at hand: eliminating all risk of being followed. Otherwise, this whole exhausting escapade would be for naught, leaving my children vulnerable once again. *Lord, give me wisdom. Show me the way.*

Inching along at little more than a snail's pace, I set my sights on the flickering of a single, stand-alone source of light. I hovered low to the ground, barely plodding along, fully aware one faulty maneuver could usher in the end.

Several minutes later, I gained sufficient distance to see what I needed to see: three figures crouching around the warmth of a campfire. Marcus and William were concerning enough, but the presence of the third man, Mr. Johnson, made my skin crawl. *Why would Marcus bring him along unless he had every intention of following through with his plan?*

Refusing to give in to fear, I continued my slow trek. Somehow, I managed to slither through the underbrush without drawing attention to myself. Once I had placed a safe distance between myself and the men, I quickened my gait.

The darkness engulfed me, making it nearly impossible to find my way. If not for the compass, I would be doomed to a night separated from my children. *Lord, thank You for this compass and for giving me the insight to bring it with me.*

Beat up and weary from my nighttime excursion, the area of woods housing the old, abandoned cellar finally came into view. My children were within reach. I willed myself to remain quiet, to keep a steady pace, to be alert. I had come too far to mess things up now.

Once certain I was alone, I slipped behind the shrubbery and made my way to the cellar entrance. The air was cold. The night, quiet. Too quiet. *Was I too late? Had they been found? Were they roaming around, looking for me? Had something terrible happened to them?*

My trembling hands reached the door and fumbled with the latch. Pushing my way inside, I feared what I might find as much as what may not be found. The outside darkness had created an even darker nemesis within the windowless structure. Eyesight was of no benefit.

Barely above a whisper, I began calling out to my children. *Clara! Roger! Clara!* No response. I whispered louder. Still nothing. With each empty response, my hope floundered. *Maybe they were sleeping.* Positioned on hands and knees, I scoured the cellar's interior until I felt confident nothing remained untouched.

Forgetting about Marcus and his men, I shot out of the cellar. *Had the children left the cellar in search of me?* I passed over the rocky ledge once more, this time without concern for anyone but my children. *Could they have fallen?* When I neared its end, I jumped to the ground and walked the full length of it using my hands as a guide. *What if I stumbled upon them in the dark? What if I grabbed hold, only to find them lying crumbled and lifeless? Sophia, you mustn't think like that! You must not lose hope! Oh, dear Lord, where are my children?*

CHAPTER 10

Where Are the Children?

I t had been two days since I had foolishly left my children alone in that empty cellar. Two Days. And I had yet to find any trace of them. No footprints. No lost garments. Nothing. They'd simply vanished in the night. *What had happened to them?*

Scared of wandering too far in any one direction, I had no idea which way to turn. *What if they had gone the opposite way? Should I stay put? Should I move on?* No matter how much I tried, no matter how long I looked, I feared I would never see my children again. And though my current reality looked as if that may very well be the case, I would never stop looking. *Oh Lord, won't You please help me find them?*

Walking. Searching. Hiding. This had become my life. I worried Marcus and his men might find the children before I did. I worried they had already found them. *Should I allow myself to be captured so I'll know for sure? And what if Marcus is not responsible for their disappearance? Allowing myself to be captured would leave the children with no hope of rescue. Then what?* I rested my head in my hands. It had all become an endless loop of worry and fear.

I continued under the cover of the woods as far as it would take me. Rather than stepping into the clearing, I sought out a nearby cluster of trees. Looking around once more, I stooped down and crawled beneath low-hanging limbs into a thick and luscious underbrush. *I must lie down, if only for a minute.*

My body needed a respite from the weariness beating against it. A few moments of stillness would serve as a good antidote. My muscles relaxed, an almost visible tension lifting from them. My thoughts fluttered about in no particular order.

What if snakes and spiders are holed up in this place with me? Am I hidden well enough that Marcus won't see me? God, watch over my children. Clara. Roger. Are they safe? Where could they be? How long until they're found? How long until they're in my arms again? How long until I can finally sleep?

* * *

I'm not sure how long I slept, but I was certain it had been too long. *How could I be so irresponsible?* Dragging my children into the woods. Leaving them alone in an old cellar. And now falling asleep with them still wandering about in the unknown, likely in harm's way. *What kind of mother had I become?*

I took a quick inventory of the backpack I had left with the children in the cellar. The children's uneaten sandwiches taunted me. Though unrelenting hunger continued to grab at me, I could not bring myself to eat the sandwiches I had prepared for them. I would find them and when I did, they would need something to sustain them.

That was something that continued to nag at me. The children had disappeared, but the backpack and everything in it had been left behind. Though Clara was young, it was not like her to leave behind something so important. *Why had she not taken it with her? How would they make it with no provisions?*

Making my way out of the thicket, I lifted my backpack onto my back while slinging Clara's over one shoulder. The sun stalled directly overhead, reminding me a decent amount of daylight remained. Taking a single step forward, I froze in my tracks—a bear, merely yards from me.

The bear stared at me blankly, looking as if I had interrupted an early slumber. Its movements were slow and methodical and not at all threatening. Raising its heavy body into the air, it limped toward me–seemingly more out of curiosity than mischief. *Could this be the same bear that chased Marcus and his helpers away? Was their gunfire the cause of the bear's limp?*

Although the bear didn't seem to pose an immediate threat, I still felt it wise to create distance between us. Being careful not to turn my back to the bear, I ascended halfway up the nearest ledge. I knew I'd have little luck in out-running it should it decide to go after me, but I had to try. Forcing myself to not look back until reaching the top, I surprised myself at the speed in which I reached it. Once there, I mustered the courage to peer below. As I suspected, I was not being hunted. The bear had lost interest, barely glancing back as it made its way toward the wood's edge. Something about the poor, injured creature tugged at my heart. *Had God sent that bear to distract Marcus? To help us get away from him and his men? Maybe even to steer us toward the safety of that old cellar?*

Amazed at the possibility of God doing such a thing, I climbed atop a large boulder and looked out in all directions. *Lord, where should I search today?* It felt useless to keep looking, but I couldn't bring myself to stop. And though I couldn't bear the thought of not searching, I also couldn't muster the strength to move. Devastation covered me like a weighted blanket. The harder I kicked at it, the more entangled I became – unable to free myself, unable to shake the paralysis overcoming me.

My legs gave way; my body followed suit. I slid down, leaning against the large boulder I had once stood upon. There I lay, in broad daylight, hidden from view by nothing but this misplaced boulder. I couldn't force myself to continue.

My mind rested on my circumstances. My heart cried out for my lost children, for the lost me who had nothing left to give. No more plans. No more hope of figuring this out. No more strength to keep walking and searching and hiding. No more strength at all. I was done. I had come to the end of myself. And I still hadn't found my precious children. *Lord, how can I go on without them?*

* * *

I lay motionless as if life itself had abandoned me. Truth be told, I would've almost rather been dead. At least then, this pain and hopelessness would not be ravaging my heart.

Poisonous thoughts stabbed at me. *Look at the terrible life you've given your children. On top of everything else they've endured, now you've abandoned them and left them for dead. Some mother you are!*

The words stung. Though deep inside I knew they couldn't all be true, I was in no position to call them out as lies. An enemy far greater than Marcus had me pinned. This enemy was called Satan. I had heard mention of him as a child, but had never thought much about him. No doubt he had joined forces with Marcus. Together, the two of them had drained all sense of hope from me and without hope, there was nothing left to do but give up.

I opened my eyes and looked toward the sky. *God, are You there? Are You watching? Do You even care?* I was unaware of the tears flooding my cheeks until the taste of them met my lips.

Oh, God! I cannot do this anymore. I have nothing left. No ideas. No solutions. No strength. No way to save my children. No way to save myself.

God, won't You please help me?

Portions of bible verses began to replay in my mind like an old movie reel. Could it be the truth I had learned in those Wednesday night services had somehow stuck with me? Could it be those truths had been a part of me all these years, simply waiting to be remembered?

You will call upon me and come and pray to me, and I will listen...

They cried out to the Lord in their trouble, He saved them...

He will save the needy when he cries for help... and him who has no helper.

I rolled over, hoping to muffle the deluge of sobs coming from my limp body. *God, You knew all those years ago that I would need those verses today. I am the one in trouble. I am the one crying out to You. I am the needy one who has no helper. Oh God, won't You please be my helper? Won't You please save me? Won't You please rescue my children? We have no one but you, God. Please help us. Please help us. Please ...*

My eyes closed. For the first time in what seemed forever, my sleep ushered in pleasant thoughts. Clara, dancing and twirling like an angel, her beautiful white gown flowing with each motion. Roger's big smile, fading in and out until its warmth enveloped me. Cradled in the shadow of that big rock, I found rest. I no longer felt alone. God was with me. Even better than that, God was with my children—wherever they may be.

Though darkness surrounded me as I slept, it didn't have a hold on me as it had hours earlier. I laid there in the quiet of the night. My mind felt an unexplainable calmness that I had never before experienced. Could this be the peace my mother had once spoken of?

My circumstances had not changed. I was still in danger. My children were still lost. But the paralyzing fear I had been carrying around had lifted. I felt an assurance I couldn't explain. An assurance that told me we would be okay. Even if things didn't turn out as I hoped. Even then, we would be okay.

CHAPTER 11

Praying for Rescue

As evening turned into dawn, the sun showcased its brilliance in vivid colors across the early morning sky. The fresh, brisk air acted as a soothing balm to my lungs. Each breath gifted renewed strength into the layers of my being. I stood erect, stretching my arms high into the air. Bending at the waist, I allowed my lower body a much-needed stretch. My muscles came alive as my spirit had hours earlier. For the first time in a long time, hope stirred within me.

My thoughts were interrupted by what sounded like the laughter of a child. *Could it be?* I cocked my head to one side while scanning the area surrounding me. It was then I noticed them; Marcus and his two companions stood a good distance from me, close enough to notice any sudden movements. I faced them; they faced the direction of the laughter. *Had they heard it too? Could they see what I could not?*

Fearful of drawing attention to myself, I remained motionless. There it was again! It *was* laughter! And not just any child's laughter; it was *my child's laughter*.

Clara's sweet laugh! Oh, how I feared I would never hear it again.

But now what? I wanted to run straight toward the sound, but would I place the children in danger by doing so? Should I wait on Marcus to make his move? What would he do if he made it to them before I did? My heart nearly burst from the despair building up inside.

Then I heard a subtle reminder, a gentle whispering within my spirit.

"Sophia, I Am here."

Oh Lord, it is You! What would You have me do, Lord? I cannot fight this battle alone. I cannot protect my children without Your help. Please shield them, Lord. Protect them as only You can. Give me wisdom and strength to face the struggle ahead. Help me, Lord, to listen and obey. Help me, Lord, to trust You.

It was killing me to stay put, but one wrong move could ruin everything. I coerced myself to remain in the same spot. Minutes seemed like hours. Finally, the sun cast a deep shadow, its reach stretching upon the ledge standing near me. I inched to the right, slowly and steadily, my gaze fixed upon the men whose gazes appeared to be fixed upon my children.

After several moments of inching along, I made it out of the clearing and into the tree line. From this angle, I began to notice familiarities in the landscape. By following the tree line, I should come upon the open area near the old cellar. *Could it be the children had been this close the whole time?*

No longer able to restrain myself, I sprinted through the wood's edge, bent on intercepting my children. I could not see Marcus from this angle but could not risk him reaching the children first.

Nearing the cellar's vicinity, the children's voices gained clarity. Clara was singing. Roger was chattering away, about what I wasn't sure. I heard squealing and giggling, the beautiful sound of childhood and all things happy.

Then I detected a third voice. A man's voice. Though muffled, he sounded gentle and kind and somehow familiar. *Who was this man? Where had he come from? How had he ended up with my children?*

As the children came into view, so did the three men intent on capturing them. The scene unfolded quickly, but it felt as if it were in slow motion. Clara spotted the men advancing toward them. She rushed to Roger's side and wrapped him in her small arms, desperate to keep him safe.

A scream escaped my lips, "No!" *Lord, help us!* The caretaker of my children looked my way. His eyes, filled with compassion. I had seen that same compassion in those same eyes so many times. *Daddy?*

He stepped in front of the children at the same moment I reached their side. Marcus and his men pressed upon us. But this man I had hurt so badly—he stood firm, shielding the three of us from the three of them.

"You have no business here, Marcus." He spoke with firmness and authority.

Marcus glanced from us to our protector as if to weigh his options. *Did he not realize this was my dad?*

Marcus pushed forward once more, taking a swing at his older opponent. At the same time a man rushed from behind us, grabbing Marcus's arm mid-swing and throwing him to the ground. William ran toward the man and attempted to free Marcus from his grip.

While the three of them rolled around, two more men rushed in from what I now realized must be a small home built into the side of the hill. *Did this home connect to the cellar where I'd hidden the children?* The two men glanced at my father; he nodded as if giving them approval to join the brawl. One attempted to pull William from the pile, intending to subdue him. Fighting ensued until William managed to break free, punching and kicking his assailant and rendering the man unconscious. Then William turned and headed straight toward us.

My father, still standing guard over the children and me, held his ground. He refused to give up his position. "You might want to rethink yourself, son."

William paused, looking from us to Marcus and back again. Marcus continued to put up a good fight but was beginning to show signs of exhaustion. *How had I not known he could fight so well?*

I watched in frightful expectation. *Would Dad be strong enough if William persisted? Should Marcus break free, how would Dad fight them both off? Would he be forced to hand us over? Would he be harmed in the process? God, be his strength. Fight this battle for us.*

It seemed as if William had somehow heard my silent prayer and knew he was fighting a battle he could not win. He locked eyes with my dad a moment longer, glanced back at Marcus who had all but lost the upper-hand, and then fled into the woods. Marcus was left to fend for himself. *Could it be we were on the verge of freedom, and Marcus was now the one being held captive?*

It was then I remembered Mr. Johnson. My eyes darted from one man to another in search of him. *Where had he gone?* No sooner had I asked myself this question than a loud, thundering shot broke the silence. Birds flitted from the treetops. The men clamored low to the ground; all but my dad. He flinched, but quickly resumed his stance. His hand instinctively reached behind him as if to let us know he was still there. I held tighter to the children, wishing somehow the earth would open up and offer us temporary cover.

"Release Mr. Gadson at once!" Johnson spoke directly to the men detaining Marcus. They hesitated, then slowly loosened Marcus from the entanglement they had forged around him.

No, no, no! This can't be happening! God, please help us!

Both children were trembling beneath me. "Shh, it's okay; it's okay." The last thing we needed was to draw attention to ourselves. That would come soon enough.

Mr. Johnson ordered my dad's men to remain face down, while Marcus dusted loose dirt from his designer jeans. He spoke in the calm, intimidating tone he had used with my dad when we last visited my parents.

"Well, well, well. What do we have here? It seems Gramps is a slow learner." He and Mr. Johnson snickered.

Dad remained silent. I crouched behind him, eyes squeezed shut, knuckles red from gripping the children so tightly. I felt like a coward. *What had I gotten us into? How could my family ever forgive me for the mess I had caused?*

"I'm going to need you to step aside, old man."

"I can't do that, Marcus. I won't do that."

"The way I see it, you don't have much of a choice, now do you?"

I peeked around Dad, assessing our situation. Marcus motioned for Mr. Johnson to aim the gun our way. Still, Dad did not budge. If he were frightened, I couldn't tell. Nor could Marcus.

"Is this really how you want things to end, Marcus? Do you really think you'll get by with this?"

"Why wouldn't I?" Marcus barked back. Dad had struck a nerve.

"As I see it, you have quite a few witnesses to contend with. Even if you manage to kill every one of us, you'll still have the monumental task of disposing of our bodies. You certainly can't leave them strewn about here on your own property. That'd be a dead giveaway. And then there's all the evidence you'd need to cover up."

"Evidence?" Marcus laughed but there was no humor in his eyes.

"Yes, this area reeks of evidence. For starters, these men you've been wrestling with are covered in your DNA. And then there's the matter of a missing mother and her children. Once I finally figured out where you had taken them, I took the liberty of notifying local authorities of my suspicions."

"Suspicions? What suspicions? You're not making any sense, old man. I'm growing tired of your little games."

"That's okay. This little game, as you call it, will soon be over." Dad glanced at his watch as he spoke. "Your local police department should be arriving any moment now, search warrant in hand, to conduct a welfare check on Sophia and the children. When you don't answer the door, they'll pocket the search warrant and begin searching the grounds. The possibility of you holding Sophia and the children against their will is strong enough to justify them snooping around. Tell me, Marcus, how do you intend to explain the sudden absence of your wife and children when your house is filled with evidence of their presence?"

Marcus spoke through clenched teeth. "You're bluffing."

"Oh, am I now?"

I peeked around my dad in time to see Marcus and Mr. Johnson exchanging glances, bewildered by this new turn of events. *What would be their next move?*

While their eyes were locked on the three of us, Dad's men regained their composure and rushed them from behind. Another fight broke out, causing Mr. Johnson to lose his grip on the gun. I watched the gun catapult into the air, landing on the ground with a thud. All eyes fixated upon it.

My dad made a sudden dash to secure the deserted gun. Just as his hands grabbed hold of it, Marcus was on him. They both struggled for its possession much like they had struggled over us.

Lord, do something!

I considered running for the woods again or taking refuge in the house built into the hill, but was there any point in running? Gunshots jolted me back to the horrid scene. My dad and Marcus lay in a heap, blood puddling beneath the two of them. Neither of them moved.

My heart began to pound and scream within me. *No! No! It can't end this way; it just can't! Oh God, please don't let it end this way.*

The children called to me, redirecting my thoughts to what really mattered. I must shelter them from whatever tragedy had just gone down. Standing on shaky legs, I lifted the children to their feet. Intent on blocking their view, I cupped my hands around their faces as a shield. Huddled together, I steered them toward the small house and guided them inside.

I knelt low and hugged my children, careful to keep an eye on the open doorway. "Clara, I know these past few days have been hard on you, but I need you to do one more thing for me—only one. I need you to make sure Roger stays in here with you while I step outside to check on things."

Hesitation and fear clutched my sweet girl.

"Clara, I promise I will not leave this place without you and Roger. I won't make that same mistake twice. If you need me while I'm outside, just cry out and I'll be here." *Lord, please enable me to keep this promise.*

Clara nodded her head, wiped her tears, and took Roger by the hand. I watched as the two of them took their usual stance. Sitting together. Off in a corner. Roger in her lap. Her arms holding him close.

My heart broke a little more.

C H A P T E R 1 2

Hellos and Goodbyes

D read clung to me, making each step heavier than the last. *Were they both dead? Had Marcus suc-ceeded in eliminating my father's influence once and for all? Had my father—the only one who cared enough to come after me—given his life to do so?*

When I returned, Dad had been positioned a safe distance from Marcus. One of Dad's men attended to his needs. One stood over Marcus. Another guarded Mr. Johnson. A helicopter hovered above us, drowning out sirens in the distance. And I could do nothing but stand and stare.

Everything around me began to move at warp speed. The helicopter drifted lower, coming to rest in the clearing. Medics scurried onto the scene and wasted no time assessing their two patients. Their whispering and somber expressions made it obvious my father had suffered the greater injury. They worked quickly and skillfully, prepping him for his flight to the nearest trauma center. One medic placed an IV in his right arm;

another covered his face with an oxygen mask while a third checked his vitals.

I couldn't think clearly.

Where was the nearest hospital? How would I get there? And Mom...how would I reach Mom? How could I even face her after all of this?

Though I feared seeing my dad in this condition, I could no longer resist the urge to be near him. Squeezing through the sea of medics, I pressed my way to Dad's side and held his lifeless hand in mine. The warmth of his love rushed through me, followed closely by an unwelcome cloud of anguish. *How had I forgotten how much he loved me? How had I forgotten my love for him?*

A young medic leaned down, speaking quiet words over me. "Ma'am, we need to go now." I nodded, kissed my dad's hand, and watched as they wheeled him away. His eyes remained closed, but I knew what I would see if he opened them. Even now, his eyes would reflect nothing but love for me. No pouring on of guilt. No lathering of shame. Only love and concern, neither of which I deserved.

Marcus lay on a nearby stretcher, bandages covering his midsection and shoulder areas. I watched as a police officer cuffed one of his legs to the stretcher's metal bar. As they rolled him past, he glanced my way. His eyes held nothing but anger for me.

Trying to ignore his last-ditch effort to instill fear in me, I scanned the scene one last time. Gloved hands tagged the gun as evidence and carried it toward a squad car. A plethora of police officers combed the area, presumably searching for clues to connect the dots of their latest crime scene.

As I breathed in the hope of a better future, the irony of my present situation was not lost on me. *Wasn't this the heartache Dad had insisted my marriage with Marcus would breed?* His words came back to me as if they were spoken only yesterday. "You're headed straight for a crime scene with that man, Sophia! Your mother and I are begging you not to go there."

Oh, how I wish I had listened. Why had I been in such a hurry to break free from my parents? Why had I refused to see what my parents saw so clearly? They understood the ramifications of what I chose to overlook. Marrying Marcus would lead to the breaking of me. And the breaking of me would lead straight to the breaking of Dad. *I'm so sorry, Dad.*

"Sophia?"

It was one of the men who'd helped Dad.

"Yes?"

"Your dad made me promise I'd speak to you if he couldn't. He wanted you and the children to know how happy he was that he'd found you."

"How did he find us?"

"Well, after months of searching himself with no leads, he resorted to hiring an investigator. I'm that investigator. When nothing helpful turned up on a personal level, we began focusing our efforts on business entities. You wouldn't believe the number of rental companies in this region. We initially searched within a 50-mile radius, but it got us nowhere. Then we expanded our range to a hundred miles. It took a while to weed through them all, but we finally found what we were looking for. Once we narrowed the company's vicinity to a specific area, it didn't take long to track down the owners."

"I see."

"I know it's a lot to take in. When you're ready to know more, reach out to the local police department. They'll know how to contact me."

"Okay. Thank you for all you did to help my dad—to help my children and me."

"You're very welcome. And try not to worry about your dad. He's a stubborn one. I'm sure he'll be up and at it in no time." He tried to cover his worry with a cheery tone, but the glint in his eyes suggested he hadn't succeeded in convincing himself, much less me.

It wasn't until he had traveled the full length of the clearing that I realized I hadn't caught his name. Even more disappointing, I had failed to ask him the nagging question I simply could not shake. *How had Dad shown up at exactly the right time—in exactly the right spot—to intercept the children and pull off the rescue?*

The old Sophia would've chalked it up to nothing more than coincidence. But the new me felt certain there was more to it. *God had answered my prayers. God had orchestrated our rescue.* I would simply need to rest in those truths and trust that more details would surface later.

I turned back for my children, entering the house to find them exactly where I had left them. Their relief at my return was palpable. Tears spilled from Clara's eyes. Roger broke out in a silent wail. Both clung to me without abandon. I could do nothing but weep with them.

A kind officer stood behind us, patiently offering us the space and time we needed. After moments in this stance, I composed myself. After dabbing tears from their troubled faces, I gently gripped their tiny hands and lifted them to their feet.

"Mommy, why is that policeman staring at us?"

"He's here to help us, Clara. He's going to take us to a new home. One where we'll be safe and happy."

"Can we go to Grandma's house instead?"

"Not yet, sweetie. I need to talk to Grandma first."

"Will this new place have a playground, Mommy? I've always wanted a playground."

"I'm not sure, Roger. But even if it doesn't, I have no doubt you'll find a way to have fun." He grinned at the possibilities.

The officer smiled at Roger's innocence. "Ready when you are, Ma'am."

I paused, allowing us ample time to steady ourselves before making our way down the hill and into the officer's unmarked SUV. Once the children were secured in the SUV's built-in car seats, I situated myself directly behind them. I couldn't stand the thought of them being out of my reach again anytime soon.

The officer shifted his vehicle into low gear, maneuvering his way out of a grassy, makeshift parking area onto the paved roadway. Within moments, the gated entrance to our property was within view. Though the house couldn't be seen from the road, I imagined how it would look growing smaller in the rearview mirror. *Would the heartaches we'd suffered within its walls also grow smaller with distance?*

I leaned forward and placed a hand on each child's shoulder. Instinctively, both children reached up and rested their hands on mine. With my children safe, my thoughts slipped back to my parents. *What if Dad doesn't recover? What if I never get the chance to tell him how sorry I am? Oh God, please let him be okay. And what about Mom? Was she aware of Dad's plan to rescue us? Had she already been notified of Dad's condition? And if Dad's injuries take his life, will she ever fully forgive me? Will I ever be able to forgive myself?*

CHAPTER 13

In the Palm of His Hand

After a fairly short commute, the patrol car came to a halt outside a small housing complex. Aging and not at all fancy, it was clean and well-maintained. Rows of hedges, all the same height, lined the two buildings. The grass had been neatly mowed; only a few weeds remained visible in the flower bed.

My attention shifted to those I assumed were residents of the facility. Women perched on wicker chairs, chatting like old friends. Children played a game of tag in a fenced area between the buildings. A small boy and his mother smiled and waved as they strolled past. Clara returned their greeting. I did nothing but stare.

This was too much.

How could this be the way my life plays out? None of it felt right. Not life with Marcus. Not life without my dad. Not life in a woman's shelter. Yet this is where I've landed.

The officer held the car door open, waiting for us to exit. The children looked to me for instruction, but I had none to offer. Lowering my chin, I allowed my tears to fall, hoping they would wash away the fear fighting for ownership of my heart.

Lord, I am so grateful for the amazing way You rescued us. And though I'm learning to trust You more, I'm struggling to trust You in this moment. Marcus may be gone, but the mound of unknowns rising before me makes me question whether I'm truly free. Oh God, won't You pour Your peace over me now as You did then? Won't You once again make a way where there seems to be no way?

It was Clara who broke the silence. "Mommy, are you okay?"

The cool autumn air greeted me through the opened car door. I breathed it in deeply, savoring its goodness. "Yes, sweet Clara; Mommy's okay. Sometimes life feels scary—even to mommies. But I'm learning that, if I watch closely, I'll see all the little ways God cares for us."

I turned Clara's hands over until they rested, palms-up, in my own. "Clara, God holds us in the palm of His hand. He always has and He always will. That's one lesson I've learned well over the past few days." She smiled. I playfully touched the tip of her nose and then ran my hand through Roger's tousled hair. "Now, what do you say we go check out our new home?"

The officer helped the children from the car and then extended his hand to me. I may have been mistaken, but I was almost certain I saw a tear or two collecting in his eyes. I couldn't fathom how a stranger—even a public service officer—could care so much when Marcus cared so little.

We stepped out of the car and onto a new path. It was a path I hoped would propel us forward into places we had never before experienced. Good places. Places leading to the better life I had always longed to give my children. *Thank you, God, for placing us on this good path.*

"Thank you, Officer. You've been very kind."

"My pleasure, ma'am. If you'll enter through those double doors straight ahead and ask for Marge, she'll get you fixed up."

Offering him a timid smile, I thanked him once more and turned to face the building's main entrance. Following the sidewalk as far as it would carry us, we paused before entering. *Welcome to The Blessing House* hung in golden hues above a stark white door frame. Below the welcome sign, a smaller message caught my eye. Its inscription read, "Every good and perfect gift is from above, coming down from the Father of the heavenly lights, who does not change like shifting shadows" (James 1:17).

I had forgotten this verse just as I'd forgotten all the others I had studied as a child. I read it a second time. *Blessing House. Every good and perfect gift. From the Father—who does not change.* The words danced from one end of my mind to the other, dragging images from our escape and rescue onto the dance floor with them.

God, You are so good. Thank You for helping me see the evidence of Your goodness in our lives. Every good and perfect gift does, indeed, come from You. Of this, I am sure.

Though fear may chase after me, though it may sometimes threaten to overtake me, I now know where to run for help. And when the enemy whispers his battle cry over me, *"You and the children will never be free, Sophia!"*—I will choose to remember.

Lord, regardless of what becomes of us now—no matter what difficulties we face in the days ahead—Your goodness outweighs them all. Of this, I can rest assured. Of this, I am forever grateful.

The set of double doors opened before us.

"Welcome, Sophia. We've been expecting you."

Marge stepped onto the porch and wrapped me in the biggest hug I had felt in a long, long while. Leaning backwards, she kept both hands on my shoulders and peered straight past my eyes and into my heart.

"You and the children will be safe here, love. This is your home—for now, and for as long as you need."

A single tear escaped and made its way down my cheek. Marge lifted her hand and wiped it away as if she had known me forever—as if I were a dear friend, a beloved sister, or even a long-lost daughter. No one but my mother had ever wiped my tears with such tenderness. I smiled at the thought of it. *Another good gift.*

Shuffling the children over the threshold, we soaked in the beauty and calm of our new home. "Thank you, Marge, for welcoming us here."

"You are so welcome, dear. I bet you and the children could use a snack."

A look of relief came over Clara while Roger tugged at my pants leg, "Mommy, I think I'm gonna like it here."

"I'm sure you will, sweetie."

Marge gathered the children around a small table and divvied out snacks for each. I sank into a nearby chair and, for the first time in forever, breathed in true relief.

"Would you like a glass of fresh orange juice, Sophia?"

The children and I exchanged surprised glances. "Yes, Marge, I would like that very much."

Without skipping a beat, Marge grabbed a large glass and filled it to the brim.

"Our local supermarket donated three crates of oranges the other day. I promised the manager I would not let them go to waste. Feel free to help yourself if you'd like more."

My hands cupped the glass as if its contents were laced with priceless gems. Lifting it to my lips, I sipped the orange goodness, savoring every drop. When I emptied my glass at last, I reached for the plastic pitcher and poured myself half a glass more. Not because I was thirsty, simply because I could. *Oh, how I've missed the taste of freedom.*

"When you're ready, Sophia, I'll show you and the children to your living quarters. I'm sure it would do you good to freshen up and rest a bit before dinner."

"Yes, that sounds wonderful, Marge."

"Mommy, can we take a bath? We are really dirty." Roger wrinkled his nose for effect and then giggled when Clara agreed with him.

"Most definitely. But first, Marge, do you have a phone I could use? I think it's about time I called my mother."

Appendix

Should you or anyone you know need help in the area of domestic violence, please contact:

The National Domestic Violence Hotline: Domestic Violence Support
https://www.thehotline.org
1.800.799.SAFE (7233)
Text "START" to 1.800.799.SAFE (7233)

Resources by state on violence against women
https://www.womenshealth.gov

Other Helpful Resources

Healing the Soul of a Woman, by Joyce Meyer

Called to Peace: A Survivor's Guide to Finding Peace and Healing After Domestic Abuse, by Joy Forrest

No Place for Abuse: Biblical & Practical Resources to Counteract Domestic Violence, by Catherine Clark Kroeger and Nancy Nason-Clark

About the Author

Sheila Daniel is a wife, a mom, and a Mim. She and her husband, Brad, will soon celebrate thirty-four years of marriage. She has had the privilege of homeschooling all five of their children, three of which have graduated into the next phase of life. She joined the "grandma" club six years ago and is loving it! When Sheila is not busy with her family or working on her latest book project, she enjoys blogging about her experiences in the areas of faith, family and friendship. She has a heart for women and desires to encourage them through both the good and bad parts of life. Grab your favorite coffee or tea and join her in one—or even better, in all—of her writing spaces. She can't wait to meet you there!

https://faithfamilyfriendship.com
https://www.facebook.com/sheiladanielblog
https://www.instagram.com/sheiladanielwrites/